Shtetl Tales

Volume Five

Eleanore Smith

authorHOUSE®

AuthorHouse™
1663 Liberty Drive
Bloomington, IN 47403
www.authorhouse.com
Phone: 833-262-8899

Published by AuthorHouse 12/02/2022

ISBN: 978-1-6655-7746-5 (sc)
ISBN: 978-1-6655-7745-8 (e)

Print information available on the last page.

This book is printed on acid-free paper.

Contents

Acknowledgements

I wish to dedicate this collection to the memory of my parents (Bertha and Philip Kastel), to the memory of Dr. Sumner Smith, to Len Paris, my editor, to my children (Karen, David and Heidi) and their spouses, to my grandchildren and their spouses, and to my great grandchildren.

The Schmaltzberger Dilemma

The Schmaltzbergers were a good family and an integral part of the Patchentuch community. Zelig Schmaltzberger, the patriarch, was a solid citizen and a long standing member of the Mayor's Council. His spirit was always willing, but unfortunately due to certain limitations, he enjoyed little success in his endeavors. This was not because of a lack of effort, but because he was not as practical, capable or quick witted as others. As a result, many of his projects failed. Moreover, he was not blessed with a good sense of direction, and so his Sign Committee project had failed, as did his "Schmaltzberger's Schmaltz enterprise, due to a lack of practicality. Housewives did not buy Zelig's bottled schmaltz because they didn't need it, and so the fledgling business collapsed. Some might say that Zelig lacked common sense, and in that belief they would be correct. Moreover, it seemed that Zelig's tendencies might run in the family. His two grown sons, Feishal and Meshulam, on more than one occasion had to go in search of Zelig, due to their father's total lack of a sense of direction, but they, too, were not the quickest to solve a problem, even if the solution was staring them in the face.

Feishal Schmaltzberger and his wife Frayda lived in the same building as Feishal's brother, Meshulam and his wife Pesha. Feishal lived upstairs, and Meshulam lived downstairs on the first floor. Both families were close. The wives got along with one another, and their living arrangements worked out well for all concerned. The sisters in law, Pesha and Frayda, exchanged recipes, enjoyed town gossip together, and were as close as sisters. Frayda, however, had recently gained weight and suffered from chronic knee pain. Because of this she found that climbing the stairs to her second floor apartment had become a painful and arduous chore, and she was often limping and in constant pain.

"Oy, such a shleppe," she could be heard to complain as she dragged her market basket up the narrow staircase to her apartment. "Oy, Feishal," she told her husband, "the stairs are too much. They are killing me."

"Take one step at a time, and slowly," Feishal advised his wife, "and place your basket on the next step as you rest on the previous step to catch your breath."

"I have tried that," she responded, "but it is still too hard, and I don't know how much longer I can keep this up." Faigele Scheinkopf, Patchentuch's urgent care person, did what she could for Frayda, but the knee pain persisted, as did Frayda's complaints about the stairs.

At the same time Pesha, Frayda's sister in law had been experiencing her own annoying discomfort, but of a different kind. Pesha's knees and legs were in fine condition, but she had recently developed a sensitivity to noise, not really noisy noise, but a "footsteps overhead" kind of noise. Feishal and Frayda were quiet people, and yet their footsteps on the floor upstairs resonated downstairs and were heard by Pesha, especially early in the morning and late at night. No one in the family knew what could be done about the situation, and so had nothing to recommend. When the problem reached the ears of Zelig, he also didn't know what could be done. There appeared to be no solution to the problem, and so Frayda's knees continued to ache, and Pesha continued to be bothered by unavoidable footsteps above her head.

After weeks of frustrating discussion regarding the problem of the stairs and the footsteps, the issue was brought to the attention of Rebbe Benny Rachmanes, for whom the solution was a simple one.

"Simply exchange apartments," he told the Schmaltzbergers, "and you will solve your problem," and so that is what they did. Feishal and Frayda moved downstairs, and Meshulam and Pesha moved upstairs. Zelig and his sons couldn't understand why they had not thought of this solution earlier, but in the end it all worked out to everyone's profound satisfaction. Sometimes, when a family problem cannot be solved within the family, an outside opinion can be very helpful, and in the Schmaltzberger case, it took a Rebbe.

Zelig's Bagels

At about the same time that Zelig's children were experiencing problems with stairs and overhead noise, Zelig was experiencing a problem of his own, and it concerned bagels. Zelig Schmaltzberger loved to eat bagels, and whenever his wife Hetty served them at breakfast, Zelig was a happy man. Now that he was older, however, and had fewer teeth in his mouth, he found eating his favorite bagels to be a challenge. His jaw hurt when he bit into and chewed the bagels, and each time he did, he knew he ran the risk of breaking another tooth. Hetty considered several options, and she thought it might help if she cut the bagels into small pieces that she could then warm in the oven before serving, or she could slice the bagels sideways in order to create thin bagel halves, or she could even ask Shia Fartumel, the baker, to bake especially thin bagels for Zelig.

"There must be something we can do to make it easier for you," she told her husband, who continued to eat his bagels despite the risk to tooth and jaw. He could not bear the thought of giving them up altogether, but when one day he broke another tooth he worried. What would he do if he lost all of his teeth? Then what? It seemed that the only option would be to dream at night in his bed, and imagine himself chewing on a nice fat bagel. Then he would be happy, he thought.

One day Hetty had an idea. She understood that Zelig's bagel deprivation was making him unhappy, and she decided to do something about it. She bought a couple of bagels from Shia Fartumel, and she experimented. She sliced the bagels very thin, coated them with butter and oil and then sprinkled them with a little salt. She even rubbed the bagel slices with garlic and put them into the oven to toast, after which she took a bite. To her surprise they were quite tasty, and when she served them to Zelig, he was pleased. They had a crunch, but were not difficult to chew. He would still, however, have to be careful of his remaining teeth. He could always dip the pieces into his cup of tea to soften them up. Of course, they were not quite the same as the real thing, but they made him happy, which made Hetty happy.

Soon afterward, the news of Hetty's bagel experiment spread from housewife to housewife, and it did not take long for crisp, tasty bagel slices to appear on the tables of many of Patchentuch's residents. Who then can say, with any degree of certainty, that bagel chips were not invented in the little shtetl of Patchentuch which existed a long time ago in the backwater of nowhere.

An Entrepreneur's Paradise

A long time ago, and now only in the memory of a few, a small village called Patchentuch existed somewhere in a remote and now mostly forgotten corner of Eastern Europe. To the untrained eye this seemingly inconsequential town was just another small village, one of many in that part of the world. If truth be told, however, Patchentuch was an entrepreneur's paradise. The town's inhabitants never knew or understood that they were on the cutting edge of innovation, but they were. Just for the record, credit and attribution must be given to those enterprising residents of Patchentuch who had unwittingly left an indelible mark on the lives of so many.

One of Patchentuch's first innovative citizens was the blacksmith, Oyzer Schmaltz, who unwittingly invented the toaster when he toasted his piece of plain bread, held in a set of tongs over a fire. There was also the barrel maker, Yasher Koach, who invented the shower when he cut holes in the bottoms of barrels which he then suspended from the ceiling with ropes, releasing water through the barrel's holes with additional ropes and pulleys. Bagel chips were invented by Hetty Schmaltzberger, and Shmuel Shimshack discovered baseball when he allowed the children of the village to hit around stones with his wooden leg…and the list goes on.

Yaakov Farshimmelt, the baker, established PBS (Patchentuch's Benevolent Society) when he regularly donated challas to the poor, and Anshel And Avram became AAA in an effort to make life easier for travelers on the road. Velvel Scheinkopf created Velveeta Cheese, and the Barney and Bela Circus was founded by Patchentuch's own tight rope walkers, The Flying Farshimmelts. In addition, the Daily Planner was the brainstorm of Mayor Moishe Kapoyer, in order that the people of his town should always be able to remember what day it was. Moreover, Star Market got its name from the ubiquitous Stars of David that adorned the produce carts in the town's central Market Square.

Quite often the provenance of our modern conveniences remains obscure, leaving people to speculate as to their origin. As far as Pretzels, Cheese-Its and Fritos are concerned, there is strong evidence to suggest that they, also, were the creations of Patchentuch residents the Pritzkers, the Chesnicks and the Friedmans, respectively, but that has yet to be determined.

Mendel Makes A Choice

When Mendel Teitlebaum, son of Shlomo (Shleppy) Teitlebaum and Malkah Leah Kishkes Teitlebaum, was a small boy, he decided that when he grew up he would become a woodsman. He would follow in the footsteps of Moishke Minevitz and Zion Lochinkopf, who were also woodsmen, and whom he admired.

"So a banker's son should become a woodsman?" the yentas were heard to ask. "Is this a dignified profession for the son of the head of The First Nashamal Bank of Patchentuch?" they asked one another, and anyone else who might have an opinion. Mendel's own mother, Malkah Leah, was not particularly thrilled with Mendel's choice of career, but his father Shlomo (Shleppy) felt it was an honest way to make a living, and if that was his son's choice, so be it.

As Mendel grew into manhood, even the grandfathers had opinions regarding their grandson's career choice. Schmendric Teitlebaum, Mendel's grandfather on his father's side, and Abraham Kishkes on his mother's side, had their own ideas. Even Kasha Varnishkes, Vov Lochinkopf's, father in law, also had an opinion, as if anyone cared. It appeared as though everyone in Patchentuch had something to say regarding the future of their banker's son.

"A banker's son should become a woodsman?

Anyone can chop wood," some said. "A banker's son who has brains, which Mendel has, should not waste his life chopping wood."

Everyone in the village understood that occasionally there were "renegade" sons like the Farshimmelt twins and Moishe Walensky who went off to join the circus, but traditionally, Patchentuch sons followed in the footsteps of their fathers, as they were expected to do. Granted, there was a constant need for wood in order to maintain life in Patchentuch, or anywhere else for that matter, but the son of a banker should chop wood? Eventually, what should have been a private family matter became the business of the entire town, and a matter for serious discussion. Similar issues had arisen in the past when sons defied the traditions of their fathers and struck out on a different path. It was not a new phenomenon, but one which demanded an opinion once it became public.

"Are you implying that woodcutters have no brains?" some asked.

"No," was the answer, "but bankers require a special kind of brains, which Mendel has."

"So how can you be sure that Mendel has inherited these special brains?"

"Everybody knows that Mendel has the brains of his father, and the father has the special brains a banker must have if he is to properly serve his community."

"So, if you have these special kind of brains you can't chop wood, if that is what you want to do? Must you have the special brain of a woodcutter to be a decent woodcutter," and one would think that the residents of the town might have better things to do than to discuss the merits, or lack thereof, of becoming a woodcutter.

In spite of all past experience that this weighty subject would be just another discussion without resolution, talk nevertheless continued among people whose business it was not, and the yentas, especially, were loving it. In the end, however, Mendel's wishes prevailed, and instead of becoming a banker, he chopped wood along with Moishke Minevitz (whose own father had had a different profession in mind for his son.) It all worked out as it should, and Mendel was happy not to be required to sit behind a desk working with accounts and figures for the rest of his working life. The town residents continued to have a ready supply of wood, and life in Patchentuch continued as it always had, and, for the most part, sons continued to follow in the footsteps of their fathers, always with exceptions, of course.

Over The Rainbow

Many in Patchentuch were surprised when the Brutskis sisters, Basha and Bayla, married the undertakers, Gimpel Rozencrantz and Farmisht Blum, respectively. No one thought that these maiden ladies would ever marry, but they had, and in time a son was born to each couple.

Both undertakers, Gimpel and Farmisht, were great admirers of the Yiddish writer, Yitzhak Leybush Peretz, and so when their sons were born, each named his son after the great man. Gimpel gave his son the name Yitzhak, while Farmisht named his son Leybush. In this way they were able to pay homage to the luminary whom they so much admired. Moreover, when their sad work became overwhelming, these two members of the Burial Society escaped through their books. They transcended the lonely sadness of their work, and in their imagination flew somewhere "over the rainbow". Unlike the Flying Farshimmelts who had left Patchentuch to join the circus, Farmisht and Gimpel had dutifully remained to follow in the footsteps of their fathers, who had spent all of their working lives burying the dead of the town.

As Yitzhak and Leybush grew into young manhood it appeared to one and all that they had inherited their fathers' love of books and literature. They, too, read the works of Y.L Peretz, especially enjoying the tale of Bontsha Schweig, (Bontsha The Silent) which, as it turned out, became the template for their own lives. The symmetry was unmistakable, because, like Bontsha, the sons never complained about their own stifled dreams, but accepted their fate in silence. They never ran away to join the circus as had the Farshimmelt brothers, and they never flew "beyond the rainbow." They never ventured beyond the boundaries of their little shtetl, and only in their imagination were able to transcend the restrictions that the reality of their sad, but noble lives imposed. It appeared that the sons were heir to the stifled dreams of their fathers, and to the silent longings of Bontsha Shweig and all those others who remained in the shtetl, never to fly "over the rainbow."

A Refresher Course For Pinchas

Schlamazel Lifshutz, the schnorrer of Patchentuch, was known among other schnorrers of the region to be being eminently successful in his chosen profession. Indeed, Schlamazel himself, had mentored others in his chosen line of work, regarding how to improve their own techniques. Shlamazel had, for example, thought he had been successful in mentoring Pinchas Dumkopf, the schnorrer of the neighboring town of Schmertzburg. Of Pinchas, Schlamazel had been proud…at least for awhile.

It seems that Pinchas had recently embarrassed himself at one particular Bar Mitzvah celebration when he demonstrated extreme gluttony by stuffing his newly enlarged coat pockets with so much food that the host of the affair was called upon to chasten the schnorrer in public, actually requesting him to leave. The whole affair was so disturbing and humiliating to Pinchas, that the distraught schnorrer paid a hurried visit to Patchentuch to see his old friend and mentor, Schlamazel Lifshutz.

It appeared that during their initial schnorring lessons, Schlamazel had taught Pinchas many things regarding the improvement of his schnorring techniques. He had counseled Pinchas about washing his clothes, as well as taking a bath once in awhile. He also suggested to Pinchas that he not attempt to conceal his missing teeth out of vanity, but expose them when he smiled in order to evoke pity. Schlamazel had explained the need to demonstrate humility and modesty, qualities essential for a successful schnorrer, but apparently he had not sufficiently emphasized the part regarding moderation versus excess, or Pinchas had just forgotten all about it. If so, then the resulting unfortunate incident of the over stuffed pockets was inevitable.

"What did I do that was so wrong?" inquired a visibly distraught Pinchas of his former mentor?

"What did you do wrong?" Schlamazel asked. "I'll tell you, you dumkopf, what you did wrong," replied an exasperated Schlamazel. "You are a chazzer, a pig, who understands nothing of moderation. You apparently lack the deftness, the taste and the common sense and nuance that successful schnorring requires," and he went on to further instruct his former student who had once shown such promise.

"I am disappointed in you, Pinchas," Schlamazel continued, "because you know nothing from moderation," at which point Pinchas hung his head in shame, and a tear fell down his cheek

After the lecture from his former mentor, a chastened Pinchas returned home, determined to improve his ways. He would not only become more obsequious than ever, but also he would never again take more than a reasonable share. He would more fully develop his schnorring techniques, and would never take more than a respectable portion of food, especially if anyone was watching. He would have his wife, Bayla, replace his newly sewn commodious pockets with smaller ones, as a reminder of moderation. In time, when he had re-established his previous respectability as the legitimate schnorrer of Schmertzburg, perhaps he would re-visit the idea of larger pockets. For now, however, after his brush- up tutorial with Schlamazel, and with the passing of time, Pinchas hoped that the unfortunate incident would be forgotten. The large coat pockets had certainly not helped Pinchas because they had seemed to cry out to be filled. For the time being, at least, he would try his best to be more discreet and pitiful, and to restore the charitable nature of the good people of Patchentuch.

Who Is Tateleh?

Some time ago Breindel Schpilkes stopped in to the herbal shop of Mendel Schmootz to pick up medicine for her father, Shmuel Schpilkes, who was suffering, yet again, from heartburn brought on by his wife Chanala's cooking. Tateleh Schmootz, Mendel's son, whom Breindel had not seen in many years, as he had been away studying in Lodz, happened to be home in Patchentuch helping out his father in the shop. The two friends from their younger days, Tateleh and Breindel, rekindled their friendship, fell in love, and were later married.

Breindel knew that Tateleh's real name was Sheldon (but that is another story), but she firmly believed that Sheldon was actually a more suitable name for a grown man, so as a result she preferred to call him Sheldon. In time, the people of the town got used to calling Tateleh, Sheldon, and the nickname fell into disuse.

When a son was born to Sheldon and Breindel, and when the time came for naming Baby Schmootz, it was decided to name him after Uncle Mordecai Schpilkes, on Breindel's side of the family. They named the baby, Morton, because Breindel believed it to be a more "modern" name than Mordecai, just as Sheldon's own name was more appropriate to the times than was the name Tateleh. The irony of the situation, as it turned out, was that Breindel was so enamored of their adorable little son, and was so taken with his charm and his lovely nature, that she began to call him Tateleh, which was really just a term of affection and endearment on the part of many doting mothers. And so, Morton became known in the little village of Patchentuch as Tateleh Schmootz, and Breindel loved him as she loved his father, the original Tateleh Schmootz.

The Prince Of The Gypsies

Since Ramona's son Mishak married Shayna Schmaltz, daughter of Oyzer Schmaltz, and became an apprentice to the aging blacksmith, Ramona missed her son's help in running the tea shop. As a small child Ramona had apparently wandered away from a Gypsy caravan that had camped overnight outside of Patchentuch on its way to Romania, and she became lost in the forest. When she wandered into the little village of Patchentuch the people of the town adopted the lost child whom they named Ramona, and she had lived there ever since, where now, years later, she ran Ramona's Tea shop in the Market Square.

When a son Mishak was born to Ramona, then a young woman, no one knew who the father was, and the boy's parentage was never discussed. When some of the children teased Mishak, he reported this to his mother. Ramona scolded the children who had teased her son, telling them that Mishak was a Gypsy Prince, son of The King Of The Gypsies, and from that time no one teased him again.

With the passage of time nobody thought about the family's provenance, but Mishak, himself, secretly considered himself to be a Gypsy Prince, son of The King Of The Gypsies, and he never had issues concerning self esteem.

Now that he was a married blacksmith, and, like his mother, was considered an honorary Jew of the town, he knew that his mother, now older, needed help in the tea shop. The Tea Shop was a long time fixture in the town, and when word spread that it might close, residents became unhappy and concerned for Ramona. Mishak, as an honorable son of The King Of The Gypsies, could not in good conscience allow this to happen to his mother, nor to the town that had always been his home. He discussed the situation with his wife Shayna, who spoke with her friend Fraidle Schmaltzberger of Fraidle's Knaidles fame, and after some discussion Fraidle suggested that she would be willing to join Ramona in her Tea Shop.

Fraidle was a wonderful cook, but now that she was getting older her entertaining days were over. Like Ramona, she did not want to become irrelevant, and so in this regard she offered to help in the shop. Together, with tea and cakes, they added a bowl of chicken soup with a Fraidle Knaidle to the menu, and as a result, business boomed. The two women were delighted, and the Prince Of The Gypsies, son of The King Of The Gypsies, was proud. He had come to the rescue of his mother, which is what a loyal and honorable Gypsy Prince, Son of a King, should and must do. Ramona's Tea Shop, which now served chicken soup with a knaidle, as well as tea and cakes, existed for many years after, to the profound relief of the people of the little shtetl of Patchentuch.

The Oracle of Patchentuch

Yankel Novotny was called "Yano", not because it was necessarily a nickname, but for another reason entirely. He frequently had a peculiar, and often times annoying way of expressing himself, and that is how the name "Yano" came to be. For example, if someone were to say to Yankel, "Fraidle's cooking is very good, but I, personally, don't think it is that good," Yankel might respond, "Ya, no". This might imply that Yankel agreed that people thought that Fraidle's cooking was very good, but he did not personally agree that it was that good, or did he mean something else entirely? His affirmative/negative answers often implied an instantaneous reconsideration of his original response, or was it just the way he spoke, and thus the name "Yano." (As far as Fraidle's cooking was concerned, by the way, Yano should know, because he, himself, was an excellent cook.)

Yes, Yano frequently had difficulty making up his mind, or else he could not instantaneously decide anything when asked. His wife would ask him if, for example, he wanted another latke, to which he might respond, "Ya, no," or a neighbor would ask for help in doing something, and Yankel would say, "Ya, no" before he could decide what he really meant to say… but you get the idea.

Yankel was a cook by profession, and one might ask why the town of Patchentuch would ever need the services of a cook, or could even pay one. Housewives cooked for their families, neighbors often cooked for neighbors, thus there was no need for a restaurant. So, also, was there no need for a cook. Who needed a cook when everyone cooked for themselves and their families? As for cooking instruction, women exchanged recipes and girls learned to cook from their mothers at an early age, and if there was no need for a cook in Patchentuch, then how did Yankel earn a living? As it happened, Yano was a spectacular cook who could create tasty and wonderful dishes for which no one had the recipe. Everyone knew that he had learned to cook his exotic and amazing dishes from someone, somewhere, somehow, but who this someone from somewhere, somehow was, remained an unexplained mystery. Yano's dishes were one of a kind, and when the people of Patchentuch tired of eating black bread and herring, they might save their zlotys to buy a special dish from Yano.

When Mayor Moishe Kapoyer came out of retirement for the third time, the people of Patchentuch were so happy that they decided to arrange a celebration to mark the occasion. Life in their village was hard, and when an occasion arose that called for a celebration, the people celebrated. The time of the yearly Purim Shpiel was such a time, and the fact that their Mayor had returned to resume his official role was another such time.

It was decided by the Celebration Committee that voluntary donations would be accepted for the party, and with the money collected, they would engage the services of Yano to prepare some special delights. A member of the committee approached Yankel and asked him if he would be willing and available to cook some special dishes for the occasion. In typical Yano fashion he answered "Ya, no," and the committee member took this to be a "Yes." For a split second Yankel had forgotten that he would be away that weekend, and could not oblige the committee, despite the fact that he would have done so it if he could have, and so plans went ahead, which included Yankel's special dishes. Of course, on the day of the festivities Yano and his culinary delights were a "no show," but despite the mixup there was plenty of other food that had been prepared by the housewives of the town, as was their wont, and the celebration was a success. When later Yankel was asked about the mixup, and if everything was alright with him, and if he had remembered about a commitment to the committee, in typical Yano fashion he responded, "Ya, no," and that was the end of it. No one understood what he meant, nor could anyone cure Yankel Novotny of this annoying habit. If one would ask Yankel if he wanted to be cured, his answer would surely be, "Ya, no," and so would Yankel remain the "Oracle of Patchentuch"... yes or no?

Chatchkel Is Hungry

For many years Chatchkel Pulkes had worked for his uncle Yasher Koach making barrels. Chatchkel was not the brightest of young men, but he was pleasant and good natured. He was strong, willing and able, and was good at what he did to earn a living. He was also now at an age when most young men of the town were already married. Chatchkel, however, was supremely content without a wife, but not so his mother Hodel and his aunt Hunka.

The undertakers Gimpel Rosencrantz and Farmisht Blum had believed themselves to be happy bachelors until the time that the yentas suggested to them that they were really not. The yentas had then gone to work to arrange a shiddach for the two men with the Brutskis sisters, whom they eventually married.

"Sometimes men need to be reminded," said the yentas, "that they are not really happy, and that something in their lives is missing," but such an idea had not yet occurred to Chatchkel Pulkes. He needed to understand that he was not fulfilled, complete and happy, and so his mother and his aunt hatched a plan to educate him.

His mother suggested to his aunt, her sister in law, that she was making things too comfortable for Chatchkel by continuing to serve him such good lunches and little snacks while at work for his uncle. Likewise, Hodel, Chatchkel's mother, although it nearly broke her heart, would no longer prepare tasty meals for her son when he was at home, nor would she put food in a bag for him to take with him to work. She would serve her son bread and herring instead of what he was used to. It was a conspiracy of love and concern, because mothers and doting aunts would not always be around to care for their sons and nephews.

Eventually, after receiving sparse meals at home and at work, Chatchkel began to realize that perhaps this is what wives were for. They were there to make things comfortable for their husbands by feeding them properly, and so Chatchkel's awareness began to grow. He could no longer depend on his mother and his aunt to adequately feed him, and so, one day, when he was very hungry, he had a talk with Hunka, his aunt, who explained to him that, yes, indeed, that is what wives were for. Whereas Chatchkel liked to eat, and he enjoyed his food, he would have to find a wife, because that is what wives did. The purpose of a wife was to provide comfort, but especially food for her husband, and to this end Hunka had a talk with her friend Shprintze Shmookler.

Shprintze, herself, had married Label Perlmutter later in life, and, if truth be told, he had married her because of her cooking. Coincidentally, Shprintze had an unmarried niece who, like her aunt was a good cook. Her name was Dvorah Shmookler, for whom the family had abandoned all hope of marriage. Dvorah had little to recommend her, aside from her cooking, and because Chatchkel was hungry for good food, the two were introduced, and eventually they married.

Although neither of them was a prize, they complemented one another. Chatchkel loved to eat and was always hungry, and Dvorah happily fed him. After all, isn't that what wives were for, to keep their husbands well fed and happy. After only a short time, the couple realized that they were soul mates. Chatchkel, never a small fellow to begin with, began to physically resemble one of the barrels that he made, but he was never happier.

Geshmak's Obsession

Geshmak Feinkochen was obsessed with the imagined "competition" between his town of Patchentuch and the neighboring town of Schmertzburg. In his mind Patchentuch must never be allowed to lag behind Schmertzburg in any way, and he believed that Patchentuch maintained an edge and always must. It boasted a Mayor and a library, neither of which Schmertzburg had. As far as the number of wells in each town, it was a tie, and in Geshmak's mind their neighbors must never be permitted to best Patchentuch in any way. Everyone in the town was familiar with Geshmak's obsession with the "competition" between the towns, but no one, except for Geshmak, payed any attention. They considered it a light hearted joke, not to be taken seriously. Of course there were always those in town who liked to think they were superior to their neighbors, but Geshmak made a career of it.

One day when some men of the town waited in Geshmak's optical shop to be fitted for eyeglasses, the casual subject of the "competition" came up when Leybush Blum, an undertaker, mentioned Schmertzburg. Knowing about Geshmak's "obsession", Leybush asked,

"So, Geshmak, what in our town do we not have today that Schmertzburg now has?"

"Absolutely nothing," Geshmak immediately responded, and he would know because he kept score. "Nothing at all, thank God," he repeated with emphasis.

Chaim Kapoyer, the son of the Mayor, one of those waiting for an eyeglass frame adjustment, overheard the remarks.

"I know for a fact," he joined in, "that Schmertzburg does not have a lawyer."

"But neither do we in Patchentuch," said Yitzhak Rozencranz, the other undertaker and partner of Leybush Blum."

"So for what would we need a lawyer?" queried Leybush. "We have a Rebbe and a Mayor, and if a dispute were to arise, either or both could resolve it as they have always done."

"This is true," replied Chaim, "and so there are already two reliable opinions should such a controversy arise. "However," he added, "when you think of it, although we have two excellent sources of opinion here in our town, perhaps, in addition to the one opinion according to Jewish law, and the other according to municipal and secular protocol, perhaps we need a third neutral opinion to arbitrate between the two, if they disagree."

"This could happen, now that you mention it," agreed Leybush. "We really should have a third arbitrator to carefully consider all the evidence and then to make a final judgement."

"For that," piped in the now overly excited Geshmak, "we would really require a lawyer. If we had a lawyer here in Patchentuch, Schmertzburg could never catch up or compete, and instead of concentrating on the eyeglasses he was fitting, Gehmak's imagination ran wild with the prospect of a lawyer in Patchentuch.

When the three men left Geshmak's the shop they continued the conversation they had innocently begun. Coincidentally, all three had remained in Patchentuch to carry on the family professions. Leybush Blum and Yitzhak Rozencranz, both undertakers, had dutifully taken over for their fathers, as had Chaim Kapoyer, the proprietor of the family knife sharpening business, but not one of them had fulfilled their own personal aspirations. All three had once dreamed of careers other than the ones that had been chosen for them by their families. Any one of them would have liked to study law, for example, but opportunities for Jews outside of the shtetl were limited. As the three men continued their conversation the kernel of an idea was born.

Soon thereafter they all began to study the law. They read books and they learned from all the books on law that they could find. In addition to their everyday work, they assiduously continued their legal studies, often together, and as time passed they became learned in the law. Eventually, they opened a law firm in Patchentuch called

"Blum, Kapoyer and Rozencrantz," and in this way, they bested the neighboring town of Schmertzburg, which had no lawyer. The three lawyers of Patchentuch, however, had to keep their "day jobs" because until there was a need for their services they still had to feed their families. But no matter... Geshmak Feinkochen, the optician of Patchentuch, was deliriously happy, and for the time being, he was satisfied.

Pinchas Plotz Is Playful

Some may wonder about the origin of several of our best known children's rhymes and games, and there is evidence that some of these simple games had their humble origins in the remote shtetl of Patchentuch.

The two young sons of Feival and Patchka Plotz were little mischief makers. The younger of the two, Yossel, was rumored to be a handful, while Pinchas, his older brother gave his teacher the "plotz." As a prankster, Pinchas was a constant source of irritation to his teacher, Rebbe Benny, because he always invented new and innovative ways to annoy him in class. Although Pinchas could be a "pest" to his teacher, to his younger brother, he was a hero, someone he looked up to and admired. In truth, Rebbe Benny considered the mischievous pranks of Pinchas to be rather ingenious and creative, but he kept these thought to himself. Pinchas was not a bad boy, he was just energetic and fun loving, and his younger brother adored him. Many times their mother, Patchke Plotz, left her older son in charge of his brother when she went out into the fields to pick berries for her tasty jams and jellies, and it was then that Pinchas would invent ways to keep his younger brother entertained and to make him laugh.

As Pinchas grew into young manhood he retained his sense of fun, good humor and playfulness, but he channeled his energies into more acceptable ways of expression. The songs and games he created for Yossel as a child remained with Yossel all of his life, and even as an adult he would recall those songs and games. People in the village loved Pinchas, and to this day the little ditties and games he invented for Yossel still resonate. When Pinchas invented them he always used the letter P (for Pinchas, of course) and many still remember the immortal words of Pinchas Plotz from Patchentuch…Patty Cake, Pease Porridge Hot and Peekaboo!

A Visitor From Lublin

A traveler from the distant city of Lublin named Shmul Leibele arrived as an unexpected guest at the Shtetl Betl of Hester Britchky. He told Hester that he was in Patchentuch to pay a condolence call on his cousin, Tzatzkale Goldhaber whose old mother, Dvorah, had recently died. As fate would have it, while Shmul was in Patchentuch from Lublin, his cousin, Tzatzkale, whom he had come to see, was in Lublin, sitting shiva with relatives.

Shmul decided to await his cousin's return, and so because his stay at Hester's Shtetl Betl would be prolonged, Hester made him feel comfortable. As long as Shmul remained in town he was invited to take meals with Hester and her husband Menachem. Hester's shvester, Esther, and her husband Lester were also invited for supper in order to make the guest from Lublin feel welcome. According to the imperative in the Jewish tradition, one must always give comfort to the traveler.

"So how is the chicken business?" Shmul asked Lester, who ran "Esther and Lester's Chickens."

"The chicken business is all of a sudden not so good," Lester reported.

"Why not so good?" inquired Shmul.

"For some reason our chickens are not laying as many eggs as they have always done."

"This cannot be good; are the chickens well?" Shmul asked, and Lester told him that the chickens all appeared healthy, but they had just stopped laying. After listening to the problems with the chickens and the eggs, Menachem began to complain about the arthritis in his joints.

"Oy," Shmul responded sympathetically. "Arthritis is not good."

"No, it is not."

"I know this because I, too, suffer from such joint pain," Shmul commiserated, "and it is certainly no pleasure."

"Pain is not easy for me to deal with," continued Menachem, who was a carpenter, "especially whereas I always have orders for wooden coffins."

"Oy, the coffins," sighed Shmul Leibele. "Sadly, it never ends."

"No, indeed, the demand for coffins never ends," agreed Menachem.

"I worry about him and his arthritis," Hester confided to Shmul Leibele. "He is not getting any younger."

"None of us is," said Shmul, sympathetically, and all nodded in agreement.

After a week in Patchentuch, and Tzatzkale had still not returned from Lublin, Shmul Leibele decided to leave Patchentuch. He said he could wait no longer. As it turned out, his stay in Patchentuch had been a pleasant diversion for the family, and they would miss the visitor's company, especially their frequent relaxed and reassuring conversations which had been positive and therapeutic. The visit had provided comfort, distraction and diversion, and they knew they would miss Shmul Leibele when he was gone. Shmul, himself, was reluctant to leave, but it was time. He could delay no longer. Hester, Esther, Lester and Menachem had made him feel welcome, and he enjoyed his stay with them in Patchentuch; they hoped that one day he would return.

A few days after Shmul Leibele's departure, an odd thing happened. The chickens began to lay eggs again in their usual numbers, and Menachem's arthritis radically improved. The strange thing about the visit was that when Tzatzkaleh returned from Lublin, and was told about her cousin's visit, she said she did not have a cousin in Lublin, and never had. When Hester told her brother Tevya Minevitz, the shadchan, about their mysterious visitor from Lublin, Tevya was intrigued. He incorporated the story in future performances, reminding those who heard it that, according to Leviticus in the Hebrew Bible, God expects us to show hospitality to strangers, because one cannot know if or when an angel of the Lord would come to visit.

Oyzer's Pastime

When the village blacksmith, the shy Oyzer Schmaltz, first courted his future wife, Hinda Flaische, the tailor's daughter, he left small and anonymous silver charms for her outside her door. He had been too shy and awkward to express his feelings for her in person, and these anonymous little gifts, which he had forged in his smithy, were the only way he knew to express his feelings.

Over the years, creating small, artistic metal and silver pieces in his shop, became a relaxing pastime for Oyzer. When they eventually married, his wife Hinda joined her husband in this pastime. They opened a small stall in the market place where they displayed and sold some of Oyzer's creations. Hinda collected colored stones for her husband to incorporate into his jewelry, and because the pieces were modestly priced, housewives with an extra zloty or two might purchase a piece. The little shop became a popular destination for the women of the town, if only to admire the small pieces of silver jewelry adorned with colorful stones, or just to see what was new. Hinda often helped Oyzer with the design, and she enthusiastically joined her husband in his little side business. Eventually, they expanded into the creation of brooches, bracelets and even necklaces. Oyzer did the melting, soldering and joining, while Hinda did much of the design and collecting of interesting stones of varied shape and color.

Over the years Oyzer and Hinda turned out pieces of jewelry never before seen in the little shtetl of Patchentuch, or anywhere nearby, for that matter. Jewelry was not a sought after commodity among the poor, as were the people of the town, many of whose residents struggled to keep food on the table. Prices were kept low so that anyone might afford a piece, and barter was often a means of commerce. Oyzer and Hinda did the work because it was an outlet for their artistic inclinations, and if they made a sale, fine. If not, that would be fine, too. For them the creation of art was exciting in itself, and provided an escape from the realities of a hard shtetl life. Just as a writer must write, a composer must create music and an artist paints, so did Oyzer and Hinda find pleasure and escape through their own work.

In the beginning the little jewelry shop had no name, but after some time the couple created a name for their small business, which they called, "Blacksmith Lovely Gems," or "BULGEMI," for short, and one time when a silversmith from Italy passed through the town and saw the pieces that Oyzer and Hinda had created, he returned to Italy where he had an idea of his own.

Today the internationally famous House of Bulgari is known for its intricate silver and stone creations which are based on the original designs created by the simple blacksmith of the little shtetl of Patchentuch, Oyster Schmaltz and his wife, Hinda.

Zelig Forgets

Zelig Schmaltzberger was not really surprised when everything went wrong on that day, which was a Tuesday, as he recalled. He had become accustomed to the fact that he was now old and had to adjust, and to learn new ways of coping with the inevitable. One day he had been young, and then, all of a sudden it seemed that he was old. It was a new place in which Zelig found himself, a place of which he had no previous experience, and that was the way he knew it would be from now on.

When everything went wrong on that particular Tuesday he did not become unduly frustrated, nor was he seriously annoyed. That's just how it was when you grew old, he thought. You didn't understand directions, you couldn't remember what you were just told, you had difficulty remembering what you were going to do next, and whatever it was, you wouldn't want to do it anyway because your body ached. This most recent episode in Zelig's life involved a simple appointment that he had, or thought he had, on Tuesday at 11:00 in the morning. He was to meet a man who was interested in buying his horse and wagon, neither of which Zelig needed any longer because of his lack of a sense of direction, which had become progressively worse, if that was possible. Why then would he now need a wagon if every time he drove it he became lost and confused.

Zelig had agreed to arrange for the sale on the road to Schmertzburg at 11:00 in the morning. Because he thought he might become lost along the way, he hadn't slept well during the night. He tossed and turned in his bed awaiting first light, and then he slept only fitfully. This was nothing new for Zelig, because whenever he had a morning commitment he didn't sleep well the night before. In order to arrive by 11:00 for his appointment he set out on the road at 9:30, just in case. He took a wrong turn twice, and had to backtrack; nevertheless, he'd wisely allowed extra time, and so although a bit frustrated, he was not overly concerned.

He still arrived early at what he knew to be the designated meeting place, but the buyer was not yet there. Zelig waited and waited, but the buyer never showed up, and shortly after noon, Zelig realized that he must have the wrong day, which was probably the following Tuesday, and so he returned home, taking a few wrong turns along the way back. His horse had also grown old, and had also lost its sense of direction, and so Zelig sighed and scratched his head, but he accepted what had now become a regular occurrence. He understood that this is how it would likely be from now on, but he was philosophical about his shortcomings, as he always had been, and he was grateful for all the good times he remembered, when he could remember.

Barucha Catches A Chill

Barucha Shem, Shlomy's wife, had caught a slight chill. It would not have been a problem, except that in Patchentuch the walls had ears, so to speak, and in such a small provincial town, where everyone knew everyone else's business, and thoughts, that were often best kept to oneself, were sometimes not. Once words escaped from the lips they sometimes took on a life of their own and traveled far and wide. Such was the case, when one day in the market place, the name of Barucha Shem was overheard in casual conversation between Ida Finklestein and Essa Bissel. It is unclear as to what the conversation was about, but when Essa mentioned to Ida the name of Barucha Shem, it was overheard by Faigele Scheinkopf, who was also shopping in the market. What Ida had told Essa when Essa inquired about Barucha, whom Essa had not seen for a while, was that all she knew concerning Barucha Shem was that, "all was now well." When Faigele heard "all was *now* well," that meant to her that all had *not* been well before "now," and so she was concerned about Barucha and her health. Had she been ill? Was she still ill, and if so, why had she not called upon the services of Faigele at her clinic?

Faigele, Patchentuch's only urgent care provider, had become a chronic worrier when it came to infection and the spreading of germs in her village that could lead to an outbreak of influenza, or worse. In fact, Essa had inquired after Barucha, only because she had not seen her in a while, and she was only interested to learn whether Ida might know if Barucha was well and if she had recently seen her. Having misunderstood the context of the conversation in the noisy market, Faigele, whose ears were attuned to shtetl news, began to wonder. She began to suspect that perhaps Barucha might be unknowingly carrying germs which could then spread to others, and could, God forbid, if not treated, lead to an epidemic.

In the Shem household Barucha had recovered quickly from her slight chill, and was once again well and healthy, but in Faigele's concerned mind Barucha might be infectious. After all, she had not visited the clinic, and so how could Faigele be certain. Accordingly, she stopped by the Shem house to inquire about Barucha, and Shlomy said his wife was taking a nap. Naturally, Faigele took that as a sign that Barucha was not well. The episode blew out of proportion in Faigele's health-obsessed mind, but not wanting to pry, she began to fear that if not treated, Barucha's condition could worsen, and whatever disease she had, might spread.

Fortunately, it never came to that, because Barucha was seen up and about the very next day. Thus, fear of an epidemic in Patchentuch was dispelled, and women continued to gossip in the market place, while others continued to eavesdrop, when perhaps they should not.

A Problem In Cheder

For years Rebbe Benny had employed an assistant to help in teaching the boys in Cheder. When the harassed teacher finally retired, Rebbe Benny Rachmanes was left with a predicament. Who would replace the assistant, and who would instruct his wonderful, (but unruly) boys. Rebbe Benny could teach the students their Torah studies, but because it would consume too much of his time, he would have to make other arrangements.

It was decided that two of the older and most gifted students would fill the position temporarily until other plans could be made. These boys, Anshul and Perchik, were serious and accomplished students who were both capable of teaching the younger boys, and so Rebbe Benny determined that until a permanent replacement could be found, these two young men would assume that responsibility.

Now there would be two teachers instead of only the one, and so the students would be divided into two groups, each being taught in a separate room by a separate teacher, one for Torah, and the other for general studies. The students would switch rooms at lunch time, and in this way each group would reap the benefit of a well rounded education. While Rebbe Benny searched for a permanent full-time replacement the newly established routine worked, and Cheder proceeded without interruption.

When it came time to switch off classrooms, however, students who left one room for the other pushed and shoved each other, and engaged in all kinds of shenanigans and "hi jinx." Relieved to be out of their chairs with their noses in books for so long, they needed relief, and changing classrooms provided it. They were, after all, only young boys, so for how long could they be expected to contain their boundless energy. Mayhem erupted each day when the time arrived for switching classrooms, and when Rebbe Benny stopped by one Wednesday morning to see how things were going, he was accidentally knocked over onto the floor by some playful students who were not looking where they were going.

Switching rooms had become too risky, resulting in an occasional bruised knee or bloodied nose, and so Rebbe Benny was forced to intervene. Instead of having the students pick up and exchange one classroom for another, an activity that appeared to provide too much opportunity for mischief, he ordered that it would be the teachers, not the students who exchanged rooms. In this way the problem would be avoided. Moreover, Rebbe Benny suggested giving the students a break at midday between classes and allowing them to go outside to run around and perhaps toss around a ball for a while. And so it was in the little shtetl of Patchentuch so long ago, that the concept of "recess" was born, an idea which exists to this very day, much to the delight of young students all around the world.

Anshul and Perchik

Anshul Altshuler and Perchik Pomerantz were star pupils in Cheder and were role models for the younger students. It was for this reason that the two scholars were selected by Rebbe Benny Rachmanes to instruct the younger boys until a permanent replacement could be found for their former, and now retired teacher. The fathers of Anshul and Perchik were both respected Torah scholars, and so it was not surprising that their sons were selected to teach the younger Cheder boys. Rebbe Benny also gave instruction, but he was a very busy man, and so Anshul and Perchik assumed most of the teaching responsibilities.

It was generally accepted that both young men would follow in their fathers' footsteps by becoming scholars, and it appeared at the time that they would. To have been selected by Rebbe Benny to teach in Cheder was an honor, and the two young men had taken the first step in what would likely become a lifetime career. Their fathers were proud, and the two scholars were highly thought of in Patchentuch. They were following in the footsteps of Patchentuch's finest minds, and not even the neighboring town of Schmertzburg could boast of having such talent in their midst.

Unknown to anyone, however, the two "scholars" enjoyed their celebrity, but they privately held other ambitions. They both studied hard, and since their early days in Cheder they had spent much of their time pouring over the ancient tomes and books. Because of their brilliance they were encouraged by their families, as well as the community, while privately they dreamed of another life. Other boys played in the street after Cheder, but not these two precocious lads. As a result, they had missed the freedom to be boys. They were prisoners of the expectation of others while they dreamed of lives that were not bound to tradition. They would have been happy to sell products in a shop in the market square where they could mingle with people and talk of ordinary things. That is not to say that they did not enjoy being regarded as "elite," and superior to most others of their age, but they privately envied the sons of shopkeepers who were allowed to be boys, and could toss around a ball in the street with others of their own age.

They knew that the Farshimmelt brothers had one day joined the circus, and Moishe Walensky had followed soon after, so one day Anshul and Perchik made a fateful and life changing decision. If others had done it, why not they. They pooled the money they had earned as teachers, and they left for America. Because of their acumen and intelligence, and with the help and support of relatives in America, they were able to rent a small stall where they sold vegetables that they purchased from local farmers. While in America they continued their studies, but their energies were mostly devoted to growing their little business. Eventually, the business became established, and under their astute management it grew, slowly at first, from a stall to a grocery market, and then into many markets.

Over the years Anshul Altshuler and Perchick Pomerantz, from the little shtetl of Patchentuch, became entrepreneurs of what came to be known as the A and P, and when, after many good years, they sold their successful business, it became The Great Atlantic and Pacific Tea Co. The two former scholars retired as wealthy men and eventually returned to their books full time. They continued to probe the mystery and depth of the wisdom that was found in these books, and they resumed their studies with a deeper and more mature understanding. Eventually, they and their families moved to Palestine, where, in the Land of Israel, Anshul and Perchik happily taught and studied together until the end of their days, doing what they were meant to do, where they were meant to do it.

The Last Knish

Geshmak Feinkochen and his wife Shprintze traveled to Schmertzburg for the wedding of Pinchas Popenheim, son of their long time friend Lazarus. After the ceremony, when they were at the table taking their food, Geshmak had his eye on the last knish on the tray. As he reached for the knish, someone beat him to it, removing the knish from the tray and stuffing it into his pocket. Geshmak turned to see who had taken his knish, and he saw that it was Pinchas Dumkopf, the schnorrer of Schmertzburg, who had taken it. Geshmak was seriously incensed by the rudeness of the hapless schnorrer, and he was angry. Apparently this person had not properly mastered the art of schnorring because he had just engaged in behavior most inappropriate for any schnorrer of taste, skill or humility. What could you expect, after all, from Schmertzburg, Geshmak thought to himself, and such behavior only reinforced his long standing prejudice that Schmertzburg was inferior to Patchentuch in every way. To make matters worse, when Geshmak had begun to reach for the last knish, Pinchas had shoved him, pushing his hand aside in order to win the prize for himself. Geshmak was so upset, that when he returned to Patchentuch he decided to do something about it. That he should be insulted by an inferior schnorrer was unthinkable, and he would not let the matter lie. He had been publicly insulted, and his honor and dignity attacked, and by a schnorrer from an inferior town, no less.

After seething for days over the incident of the stolen knish, Geshmak decided to sue the town of Schmertzburg on the grounds that they were unable to control their schnorrer, (which only proved their inferiority when compared with Patchentuch whose own schnorrer, Schlamazel Lifshutz was the gold standard when it came to the art of schnorring.) He, Geshmak, was supremely offended to think that he had been physically assaulted by this inferior schnorrer from an inferior town, and so he visited the law office off Blum, Kapoyer and Rosencrantz to sue the town of Schmertzburg for failing to control the behavior of its official schnorrer.

The three new lawyers, totally inexperienced and unskilled in such matters, looked at their first and only client. They nodded sagely, said "Mmm" a lot, and advised Geshmak that they would carefully study the law on the subject, and would look into filing a lawsuit. Geshmak was content, thinking that he had engaged three wise men, and that justice would be done. After he left, the three new lawyers looked at one another. One said, "I never heard of suing a town," and another added, "for the taking of a knish that didn't even belong to the town," and they all wondered what could be done, if anything.

When Schlamazel learned of the planned suit to be brought against the town of Schmertzburg, due to the behavior of his acolyte and friend regarding the knish, he was shocked and disappointed. He had only just recently gone to the trouble of giving Pinchas a refresher course in schnorring, and now the schnorrer had let him down. He traveled to Schmertzburg to pay Pinchas a visit in order to give him a proper scolding.

"So, old friend," he told him, "what became of humility and common sense? Why, all of a sudden you had to steal the last knish on the tray, even pushing and shoving to get it? You are a disappointment to me and a disgrace to our profession."

"Perhaps I should look for a different line of work," an ashamed Pinchas confessed, "a different profession, maybe?" and he apologized profusely to his former mentor.

"What you must do," a frustrated Schlamazel told him, "is that you must first apologize to Geshmak Feinkochen, and then apologize to the host, Lazarus Popenheim, himself. You must apologize to as many people as you can, you must throw yourself upon the mercy of all concerned, and you must be contrite and humble when you do this." Pinchas hung his head as his friend continued to excoriate him.

"Besides," Schlamazel added, "you have no lawyer to defend you in this suit, and even if you did, you could not afford to pay."

The upshot of the whole sorry episode of Pinchas and the knish, was that Pinchas, of course, did what Shlamazel demanded, the law suit was dropped, no one sued anyone, and Geshmak Feinkochen had proof at last, that his town of Patchentuch was the superior of the two, ethically and otherwise. As far as Blum, Kapoyer and Rosencrantz were concerned, they continued to wait for someone in Patchentuch to require their legal services, while, fortunately, still never having given up their day jobs.

The Tea Drinkers

Years ago, when they were younger, Gantza Macher and Gazinta Heidt dreamed of going into business together, but for a business they would need a shop. They were both handy men, so to this end they built a simple structure from wood, but although they now had a shop, they did not yet have a business. When a friend stopped by the empty shop for a chat, he gave the men a few zlotys for some left over building materials, and that gave the two men an idea. Their business would be a second hand shop where they would collect and repair or refurbish the castoff and unwanted items of others, which they would then sell, second hand. They called their business The G and G, and they collected, fixed and sold discarded second hand merchandise. Their inventory consisted of chairs, tables, lamps and other items that people always need and use in their homes. Because they quickly accumulated so much "merchandise," they rented a larger space to accommodate and display all the repaired and refurbished "junk" that they sold. Once cleaned and repaired, all the items were serviceable and usable, and because their stock was obtained for a pittance, and many times for nothing, they realized a decent profit. The two men did not make a fortune, but they earned enough money to support themselves and their families, and they were happy in their work.

Buying, fixing and selling is what they did and what they enjoyed. The G and G was always busy, sometimes more than others, and when they were not busy repairing and restoring broken furniture or polishing tarnished brass, they sat in the two old matching chairs they kept at the back of the shop and drank tea. The back of the shop was their refuge and their "office," one might say. It was where they kept their records, drank tea and ate the lunches their wives had prepared. In winter they sat in their chairs and warmed their hands by a pot bellied stove.

As the years passed, the two friends continued to buy, procure, repair and sell their used merchandise, and the shop was a popular destination for the women of Patchentuch who were always on the hunt for a bargain.

One day a customer wandered into the shop to browse around the clutter of chairs, tables, lamps, footstools and other assorted castoffs that now filled the larger space. He carefully examined this and that, and because he did not appear to be a local, Gantza, who was alone in the shop at the time, thought he might be from a neighboring town such as Schmertzburg. The man said that he was looking for some chairs, a matching pair to be exact, for his old grandparents. When he noticed the two chairs at the back of the shop where Gantza and Gazinta drank their tea and ate their lunches, the customer said he might be interested in them for his grandparents. For them they would be perfect. The upholstery was worn and stained from years of wear and many cups of tea, so they were not particularly attractive, but they would do for the grandparents, and would serve the purpose if the price was right. Gantza was not sure that Gazinta would approve of him selling their two chairs, which, over the years, they had appropriated for tea and lunch. That was part of the reason their "office chairs" had never been bought by anyone. After some discussion, the two men agreed upon a price, the sale was made, and the chairs were loaded onto the customer's wagon.

What Gantza and Gazinta did not know at the time, and never discovered, was that this particular customer who had purchased the two old chairs that had stood at the back of the shop collecting crumbs and dust, was not from the local area at all, but was an antique collector and dealer from Warsaw. The two old chairs that he bought turned out to be a collector's treasure, worth a great deal. Unknown to the junk dealers, they were a pair of Russian Neoclassic Mahogany Armchairs, upholstered in red Damask silk, that were eventually sold to a museum where they remain on display as a national treasure to this very day. Gantza and Gazinta easily found two other chairs from their inventory to replace the two they had sold, and on which they continued to eat their lunches and drink their cups of tea.

The Schmootz Tradition

When Tateleh Schmootz was a little boy, his father, Mendel Schmootz, the herbalist of Patchentuch, took him along on many of his herb finding excursions in the fields. Tateleh had a natural talent for the profession, and when one day he ate some violets that turned out to be harmless, his father concocted a soothing remedy from the plant, which came to be known as Tateleh's Violet Blend.

When Tateleh grew into manhood and married Breindel Schpilkes, she insisted her husband give up the childhood appellation of Tateleh, preferring to call him by his real name which was Sheldon. The boy had been named after his Uncle Shlemiel who emigrated to America and had changed his name to Sheldon. When Tateleh (Sheldon) had his own son, he was named Marvin after another uncle, Uncle Moishke, who had also emigrated to America and changed his name. As had been the case with Marvin's father Sheldon, Marvin was also referred to as Tateleh when he was young, but when he grew older, the Tateleh was also dropped and he became Marvin, which was his real name, after all.

Sheldon, Marvin's father, had not really wanted to become an herbalist like his father, but he had to support a family, which required an income. Mendel Schmootz's herbal remedy shop was already an established and thriving business, and so Sheldon became an herbalist, taking over the family business when Mendel retired. For the most part, that is the way it was Patchentuch. The undertaker's son became an undertaker, the baker's son became a baker and the blacksmith's son, well you know the rest. The inhospitable world outside of the shtetl offered limited opportunity for Jews, and so shtetl traditions were passed on to sons, and life continued as it always had.

Marvin Schmootz turned out to be a real innovator, much more so than his father or grandfather. He stocked the regular inventory, of course, but he was also creative and curious. He never ate violets or swallowed small pebbles, as did his father, but he discovered that, for example, bee balm could be an effective treatment for many ailments such as headaches, and he learned that the white daisy like flowers of chamomile produced a relaxing effect, as did lavender. Marvin also experimented with basil, ginger, garlic and elderberry, which he discovered could all be helpful in alleviating unpleasant physical symptoms, and as a result of his experimentation Marvin (who, incidentally was also called Tateleh until he outgrew the name), became well known and much respected in Patchentuch and beyond. He invented Marvin's Bees Knees, which was good for relieving muscle pains, Breindel's Basil Balm,(named for his mother), as well as Beymish's Basil Blend, (named for his baby son), both of which soothed one part of the body or another. Marvin's name was added to the list of Patchentuch luminaries, and his remedies are still widely used. By the way, Beymish was also called Tateleh until he, also, outgrew the name. Doting Jewish mothers could just not resist, and that is how it was, and more than likely would always remain.

The Schmootz Celebration

Marvin Schmootz, (no longer called Tateleh) was well known in the Patchentuch community for his innovative herbal remedies, and the family was proud of his success. His father, Sheldon (the former Tateleh) was especially proud of his son, and to celebrate his success, he invited the whole family to Ramona's for tea, cakes and chicken soup. Money in the shtetl was a scarce commodity, and the small celebration at Ramona's would cost Sheldon money. He didn't mind, however, for he wanted to honor his son, and he had put aside enough zlotys for the occasion. Marvin, who was pleased that his father would do such a thing for him, worried about the expense to his father. Nonetheless, he and his wife Breindel graciously accepted the invitation.

On the afternoon of the celebration the family enjoyed themselves at Ramona's. They consumed bowls of chicken soup with matzah balls, had tea and cakes, and all the while Marvin worried about the expense to his father. Nonetheless, they laughed, they cried, they celebrated Marvin, and when the story was told of how his father Sheldon, as a youngster, used to eat small pebbles and flowers, Marvin began to laugh. As a result of laughing so hard he began to choke on a matzah ball, and his face turned bright red. When Ramona came over to the table and asked if he would like a cup of water, Marvin replied, "How much?" at which point everyone at the party also broke out into gales of laughter, and some also began to choke.

Fortunately, no one suffered any ill affects from all the laughing and the choking, and Ramona provided cups of water to all, free of charge (much to Marvin's relief). The family would often recall Marvin's hilarious question of "How much?" and Sheldon continued to be proud of his son Marvin, his own Tateleh, who during his life achieved more wonderful things to celebrate, which they did.

The G Clefs

The small shtetl of Patchentuch can lay claim to fame (not fortune) in many small ways. Several illustrious names are associated with the now mostly forgotten shtetl town, but history remembers the achievements of those few. The contributions of these Patchentuch luminaries have, over the years, enhanced the quality of life for many, and the toaster and the shower are reputed to be just a couple of their innovations. As far as the world of music and the arts, the town of Patchentuch also can lay claim to the fame of musical groups such as The Glicklets, The Shaindle Maidles and The Three Faivels. Of the "G Clefs" we know little.

The twin sons of Moishke Minevitz, who were named Gershom and Gedalia, as well as the son of Shachne Koach, who was named Gideon, were all born on the same day, as were their fathers. Like their fathers, they were also known as Blood Brothers. Even as babies, when they cried their voices were not harsh or screechy, but were more like soft wails, not annoying or grating. As young boys they sang in shul or at special functions, causing those who heard them to remark that one day they would become cantors. The three boys were affectionately referred to by the villagers as The G Clefs, but as they grew into young manhood none of them really had any serious musical ambitions. They just liked to sing, which they did.

Gideon worked as a barrel maker with his father Shachne, and the twins worked with their father Moishke, as wood cutters in the forest. When they were not singing in shul, or performing at village celebrations, the G clefs invented their own songs as they worked among the trees or the workshop. One might say that the music they composed, hummed and whistled, might well have floated in the air and beyond the boundaries of their Patchentuch shtetl, but who is to say? Songs that the young men created in their heads as they worked, were hummed along by others whose ears they reached.

"Hi ho, hi ho, it's off to work we go," or "Whistle while you work," were only a couple of the melodies they composed as they spent their lives chopping wood and making barrels, and so who can say how far the tunes traveled through the time and space around and about them. One can only wonder about such things.

Essa Bissel's Decision

It was on Pussy Willow Path that Essa Bissel had met her husband, Boris Popenheim. He had been leisurely strolling through the woods with his brother in law, Zelig Shmaltzberger, when he had rescued Essa's cat that was caught up in a tree. When Boris rescued the cat and returned it to Essa, she invited him to dinner in appreciation. Boris, who loved to eat, was a "fresser." He so appreciated Essa's cooking, that sometime later, after they had gotten to know one another, Essa and her "fresser" were married.

Essa always made it a habit to travel this particular path because it was where she had met her husband, Boris, and because it led to the marketplace. She favored this route because it was where "her pussy willow tree" grew. Essa had never before seen pussy willows growing in the wild, and when she discovered this tree with furry buds festooning its branches, she was surprised and delighted. She wanted to cut off a few branches to bring home with her, but she worried that they might be poisonous to her cats.

Because other folks eventually learned of Essa's discovery, they, also came to visit the path, which came to be known as Pussy Willow Path. When the foot traffic became unusually heavy, however, ruts and potholes began to appear in the ground, and people were slipping and tripping. Workers were enlisted to smooth out the ground by laying wood planks along the way, but the work was never completed because workers were confused as to which path they were to be repairing. As the path became more hazardous, Essa did not complain, because fewer people came to visit the site, and she had the walkway pretty much to herself.

Every year Essa was saddened, when in the spring the furry buds disappeared and were replaced by white flowers and green leaves. Rebbe Benny had once told her, however, that in the fall the furry buds would return, which they always did. Essa still regretted that because of her cats she could not bring home a few branches, and over the years she developed a special attachment to "her tree," which she continued to visit and enjoy. In the fall of each year she reveled in the return of the pussy willows, and she was grateful for what she considered to be a special gift.

Essa never lost the joy and pleasure she received from nature, but she often wished she could bring some pussy willow branches home with her. She was not getting any younger, and walking had become more difficult, especially along the bumpy and uneven dirt path on which she often slipped and tripped, occasionally bruising a knee. One day, when she came to the realization that she could not maintain her frequent visits, she made a decision. She took some shears with her from the house, and she cut off a few branches to bring home.

After all the years of traipsing through the woods, tripping and falling along the way, she discovered that pussy willows were not dangerous to cats, after all, and for the rest of her days Essa was able to enjoy the company of her furry friends in the comfort and safety of her home. As for the cats, they mostly ignored them, as they do most people.

A Party For Moishe

Moishe Kapoyer loved his job. He had always enjoyed serving as the Mayor of Patchentuch, and when, on each of the three occasions when he had previously "retired," he had subsequently been compelled to reconsider. As the years passed Moishe was, of course, getting older, as do we all, and he began to seriously entertain, yet again, the decision to retire. Unfortunately, the people of the town would not let him retire, and they raised a hue and a cry whenever the suggestion was made. In fact, they were quietly planning to fete Moishe to honor his many years of devoted service. Housewives were already planning their cooking and baking in anticipation of the gala event, while unbeknown to the people, Moishe was quietly making plans of his own.

The time had come. He was old, and he was becoming increasingly forgetful, less forgetful perhaps than his contemporaries, but, nevertheless, forgetful. Moishe had emerged from each of his previous retirements, able to carry on as before, but this time would have to be the last. Moishe would not be getting any younger or more energetic; lately he had been forgetting about Council meetings and about items on the agenda, and he needed reminding more often. He had become forgetful about so many things, and it was worrisome to him. He did not enjoy growing old, and found the adjustment difficult. He had never been old before. This was the first time (and the last) and he had problems accepting all the limitations that old age had imposed. He had become increasingly, and more seriously, forgetful, a phenomenon which had undermined his self-confidence and in his abilities, and so he decided this to be a legitimate reason for him to retire for the final time. Four retirements were surely enough.

In order to impress upon his Council the necessity of his decision to retire, he decided not to hide his forgetfulness, but to freely exhibit it to the members of his Council. Moishe had indeed become forgetful, but he was not totally incapacitated in this regard. He had just become forgetful enough to justify his decision to others. To this end, more and more frequently, Moishe began to feign forgetfulness at meetings in order to lay the groundwork for his planned retirement announcement. He told Fruma of his plan, and she became a willing conspirator.

On the day of the planned celebration in his honor Moishe was nowhere to be found, and Fruma went "in search" of him. He had apparently decided to take a stroll that evening, and had perhaps forgotten all about the celebration, or had he? In the end, the Council, as well as everyone else, accepted that perhaps the time had really come. They seriously began to consider the prospects of a replacement for their beloved Moishe Kapoyer, His Honor, the Mayor of Patchentuch, and its only one ever, so far.

The Yentas Grumble

There are some who claim that the women's worldwide suffrage movement had its origins in the tiny shtetl town of Patchentuch that may have existed somewhere in Eastern Europe long ago in the backwater of nowhere. For its time, Patchentuch was an innovative place, and it is even rumored that folks in the village had invented the toaster and the bath shower. Patchentuch was a religious community in which the women and the men were separated. Exceptions, however, were made when it came to Faigele Scheinkopf, the Urgent Care provider for the town, but for the most part the traditional separation was observed and respected.

Patchentuch was nevertheless a relatively forward looking community, their medical clinic being unique in that Faigele was an institution unto herself. Her two daughters, Rachel and Leah, dealt with midwifery, and treated only women, but as for Faigele, exceptions were still made and had been for years. Faigele was Faigele, and that was that. It was where people had always gone, and continued to go for their urgent care, as well as scrapes and bruises.

"Go see Faigele," was what they said when a medical problem arose, and that is what they did. When it was rumored that Moishe Kapoyer was about to retire as Mayor, yet again, some suggested Faigele as a replacement. Many of the yentas, as well as the more progressive women of the community, continued to lobby for women's rights, but because there was only one Faigele, who declined the offer to become Mayor, the movement suffered a setback.

Life, however, continued on in the town, Moishe continued to forget things and to postpone his fourth retirement, the yentas continued to grumble, but after that, nothing much changed in the little town of Patchentuch.

Another Patchentuch Innovation

Some years ago Anshel and Avram Farshimmelt established a business involving roadside assistance for travelers. The company, originally called Anshel And Avram, changed the name to AAA, and had thrived. In an effort to succeed as had their now famous brothers, The Flying Farshimmelts, acrobats in the circus, they sought ways to improve and expand their own little business. People appreciated the services because wagon traffic on the roads was brisk in the area, as well as was a constant need for repair service. As a rule, most men tended to their own wagons, but there were others, who for one reason or another, could not. Perhaps they were old, or they had no sons to assist them, or neighbors were too busy with their own concerns to help. Whatever the case, AAA was there to provide service. Whether it was for wagon wheel repair or replacement or emergency aid required on the road, or just for directions and detailed maps, AAA was there to help, no matter the season or the reason. The parents of the men, Jakob and Shana Brocha, were proud of all their sons, and Froimke, their fifth, was the only one who followed in the footsteps of his father, Patchentuch's rope maker.

One day Anshel had an idea for expansion, which he shared with his brother. The people of the shtetl were frugal, and were always looking to conserve what little money that they had. Many grew and raised their own food, and they sewed and repaired their own clothing. What if, Anshel suggested to his brother, when customers spent their money for the services of AAA, the company kept a record of the expenditures. If, in time, a customer spent a certain amount, he would be rewarded with a paper entitling him to future discounted, or even free services. Avram thought the concept to be an interesting idea, and so they launched a program involving such discounts, and everyone liked it. It has, in fact, often been said that the program of "Frequent Flyer Miles," was conceived in the little town of Patchentuch by the original owners of AAA, who were the brothers of the original owners of The Barney and Bela Circus, the Greatest Show On Earth.

Froimke Writes

Jakob Farshimmelt, the rope maker, and Shana Brocha, the poetess, were parents of five boys. Their sons had distinguished themselves, making their parents proud, but of all the sons, it was only Froimke who had followed in his father's footsteps becoming a rope maker in Patchentuch.

Like the Blacksmith, Oyzer Schmaltz, whose avocation was jewelry making, Froimke also had a hobby. He was a writer of poetry and fiction, a talent he inherited from his mother. While assisting his father in making ropes for the people of Patchentuch and environs, he lost himself in thought of stories he would write, and he wrote about what he knew best, which was shtetl life. Froimke had been introduced to secular literature by his mother, Shana Brocha, who had, herself, been influenced by the poetess of Patchentuch, Bluma Tovah, now long gone. Froimke read prodigiously, and as he wound his ropes he dreamed up stories in his head. His wife, Pesha, encouraged him in his creative endeavors, and even though Froimke never left Patchentuch to travel the world as had his famous brothers, the flying Farshimmelts, he was fulfilled. Froimke's world, outside of his work, was the world of literature and imagination, and on one special occasion, when a well known Jewish Polish writer had traveled to the region to present a series of lectures, Froimke was in attendance.

Once at the lecture series, Froimke had an opportunity to personally meet the famous writer, to whom he gave the short manuscript of a story about shtetl life he had written, hoping for some feed back. The writer obliged Froimke, who remained in town for the lecture series. When the writer returned the manuscript he offered encouraging suggestions.

Years later, when Froimke read a story entitled "The Shtetl," by this very same author, whose name was Sholem Asch, he recognized familiar material, very similar to his own. For the rest of his life, Froimke Farshimmelt of Patchentuch took great personal pride in believing himself to have been the inspiration for one of the greatest Yiddish writers who wrote one of the most successful portrayals of shtetl life ever written.

Efsha's Idea

Sophie Rabinovitz was always pleased when her husband, Efsha, now retired for several years, left the house to meet with his old friends. The men often got in the way of their wives who were busy doing housework, and so whenever they left the house, the wives were relieved.

Efsha, Perchik, Mendel, Yossel, Bupkis, Getzel and Feivish were a group of seven old friends who met regularly. When the weather was good they sat outside in a small park and kibbitzed, and when the weather was not so good they conversed in Ramona's Tea Shop.

One day Efsha worked up the courage to share an idea with his friends. For some time he had been thinking about forming a singing group, and he broached the idea.

"So what do you think?" he asked them, after outlining his plan.

"What do you mean by a singing group?" they asked.

"What do you mean by what do I mean by a singing group?"

"Yes," answered Perchik.

"I mean," replied Efsha, "that we get together and we sing."

"You mean like a chorus?" asked Getzel.

"Yes," Efsha told him, "like a chorus, an ensemble."

"So what would we sing in this ensemble, and why?" asked Yossel.

"We would sing songs together in this ensemble, and we would make music. Maybe we could even someday perform for others the music that we would make."

"And where would we perform this music that we would make for whom, and why, asked Bupkis Scheinfeld.

"We might perform in shul, or at simchas, and maybe give

concerts in the park near the market square," Efsha told him. "What do you think?"

"Where would we practice these songs that we would sing?" asked Perchik, now intrigued by Efsha's idea.

"We could practice in the shul. That's where," Efsha informed his friends, and after some discussion and further explanation by Efsha, the men decided that it might be an interesting idea to consider.

"And what would we call our singing group?" inquired a curious Feivish.

"Well," replied Efsha, after some thought, "there are seven of us, and so we would be a septet, and in Judaism seven is considered to be a lucky number."

"How so?" inquired Perchik.

"There are many reasons, as some of you already know, Efsha explained, excited that his idea may have ignited a spark of interest. "The number is prominent in our holy Torah, for starters, including the seven days of Creation, the seven branched menorah and the seven wedding blessings, to name only a few."

"We could call ourselves "the Lucky Seven," suggested an excited Bupkis, and with that, the decision was made, and there, on that very day in Ramona's Cafe, the "Lucky Seven" was born.

The men informed Rebbe Benny about the nascent ensemble, at which point he offered them music with which they could then practice in the shul. They were now officially the Lucky Seven, and Efsha was their leader. After weeks and months of enjoyable practice, the men accumulated a repertoire of songs that they felt prepared to perform, and they were truly proud of themselves and their accomplishment. In truth, they were really quite good, and when the seven of them sang together as a group, the performance was impressive.

Spring had arrived, the weather was mild, and so, for their debut performance, Efsha selected the park. He advertised the program by posting announcements in the market square and about the town.

The posters read, "Sunday In The Park With Efsha", featuring The Lucky Seven.... and so, on that Sunday in the park, and on many succeeding Sundays, Efsha and The Lucky Seven performed beautiful music. They became minor celebrities in the little shtetl town of Patchentuch, they were enjoying themselves, as was their audience, and now that they were out of their respective kitchens, their wives were simply delighted.

The Patchentuch Players

The embers of the fire that was the "rivalry" between the towns of Patchentuch and the neighboring town of Schmertzburg still smoldered, and they remained hot enough to re-ignite the competition for supremacy between the two towns. It seems that Lazarus Popenheim, a proud resident of Schmertzburg had heard about Efsha and The Lucky Seven, unhappily informing him that Patchentuch now had a singing ensemble, whereas Schmertzburg did not. Patchentuch even had a Mayor and a library, and now this. Lazarus couldn't stand it.

Geshmak Feinkochen of Patchentuch, a principal fanner of the flames of rivalry, was a happy man, but Lazarus Popenheim, who had caught the competition bug, clearly was not. Schmertzburg was falling behind once again in the battle for supremacy, and before its standing slipped any further, steps had to be taken. To this end, Lazarus lobbied hard for a way to keep up with his neighbors in Patchentuch, and after much time and effort, he succeeded in establishing a small repertory company in the town, a feat that Patchentuch had once attempted but had failed. When Geshmak Feinkochen heard about the "Shmertzburg Theatre," the embers of the still smoldering fire sprang back into life, prompting him to quickly arrange a visit with Chochem Finklestein.

Chochem was the shadchan, storyteller and wedding jester of Patchentuch, and was experienced in matters relating to theatre, having at one time attempted to establish one in his own town. The effort had failed, and Chochem was surprised that they had succeeded in Schmertzburg. In order to try again he enlisted the aid of his old friend, Joseph Kaminski, in establishing a small theatre in their own town, despite his misgivings regarding the success of such a venture. Being retired, Joseph would surely have the available time to arrange auditions and rehearsals, time that the busy Chochem did not have. Joseph threw himself into the project with enthusiasm and excitement, grateful for something important to occupy himself during his retirement. He knew a great deal about theatre, and was eventually able to successfully organize a small group he called The Patchentuch Players. Regular folks, such as Schlamazel and the yentas auditioned, but whereas Chochem had given up in frustration, Joseph did not. His own parents, Avram and Esther, who knew and understood the dynamics of theatre, had lived in Patchentuch for many years before they moved to Warsaw to work in the profession. Joseph remained, however, but his sister had also moved to Warsaw to be with their parents, where she, too, became involved in theatre.

Due to the unstinting and persistent efforts of Joseph Kaminski, The Patchentuch Players became a reality. Joseph was able to put on a few successful little plays. The response was positive, and the entertainment that his shows provided was an anodyne to the dull sameness of shtetl life. Moreover, the theatre enabled the town to maintain a healthy edge over the neighboring town of Schmertzburg, to the profound relief of Geshmak Feinkochen, and it provided those who cared in his town with an additional claim to superiority.

Ida, the sister of Joseph, eventually achieved her own success, but in a much different way, and on a substantially grander scale. She was an actress, and over the years she developed a reputation in the Yiddish Theatre of Warsaw, becoming a luminary in the world of the theatre, and, in turn, shedding reflected glory upon her former town of Patchentuch, providing one more of the town's bragging rights. She eventually became, in fact, the grande dame of the Yiddish Theatre. Her name was Ida Kaminska.

Patchentuch On Stage

Froimke Farshimmelt wrote plays for The Patchentuch Players, along with Joseph Kaminski and Chochem Finklestein, and the little theatre group thrived. Geshmak Feinkochen was content, at least for now, that Schmertzburg could not keep pace with his own progressive town of Patchentuch, which was already becoming known in the area as a "center of culture."

In time, Froimke had the idea that perhaps they might add music to some of the plays they wrote. Whereas there existed a plethora of musical talent in the town, the writers approached The Klezmorim as well as The Glick Chicks and The Shaindle Maidles to see if they would be interested in participating.

When they all expressed interest, Froimke, Joseph and Chochem became excited at the possibility of producing what they referred to as "Musicals." When the undertaking eventually bore fruit, and was wildly successful, many people later claimed that the Broadway Musical had its original beginnings in the little shtetl of Patchentuch, but who is to say.

The folks of Patchentuch and surroundings flocked to their theatre, and attendance soared. It provided an escape for the residents of the region, bringing joy and happiness to otherwise drab and difficult lives, and the Patchentuch Players became a regular part of shtetl life. One of the most enthusiastic theatre goers in the town was Herschel Rabinovich, the dairyman who had since taken over for Leibush Liebowitz, who had retired. Whenever Herschel went to the theatre he was transported to another place where he did not have to get up early in the morning to milk his cows and to deliver their milk. So it was with the many others who regularly attended the theatre. Because the Patchentuch Players had become so popular, especially because of their "Musicals," people came from all around, (even from Schmertzburg) to attend productions. They had become trend setters, one might say, and when Herschel Rabinovich, a Patchentuch resident, invited a visiting cousin, Solomon, to join him at the theatre, Solomon happily accepted. Another regular theatre goer from Patchentuch, along with Herschel, was Shlemiel Secunda, who also invited a visiting relative, Shalom, to join him at the theatre.

Some people claim that, not only was Patchentuch the original inspiration for musical theatre, but for other future successes and achievements in that special world. The cousin of Herschel Rabinovich, Solomon, became the celebrated Shalom Aleichem, the creator of "Tevya the Dairyman" who became the legendary Fiddler On The Roof. Solomon Secunda, the second cousin of Shlemiel, became the composer of the song, Bei Mir Bistu Shain, and all of this celebrated musical achievement might never had come about except for visits to the inspiring musical productions of the Patchentuch Players, way back when.

Walensky's Son

Anshul Walensky was a Torah scholar in the little shtetl town of Patchentuch, as was one of his sons, Binyamin. Not so, Moishe, Anshul's other son who had run away to join the circus. Anshul, was an educated man who knew his Jewish history, and so he was able to derive some degree of comfort and reassurance in the knowledge that even during the time of the Romans, and since then, a long tradition of Jews in the circus existed.

Old Anshul knew about one Jewish gladiator in particular who had been captured by the Romans, according to Josephus, the historian, and trained by them to be a circus gladiator. His name was Shimon ben Lakish, known as Reish Lakish, who survived the ring and eventually became a free man who turned his life around to become a Jewish scholar. This knowledge provided hope to Anshul, father of Moishe, the Flying Walensky, his "renegade" son who walked the high wire.

Anshul also knew about Moyshe Shtern, now known as Tahra Bey, who performed in the Warsaw Circus by piercing his body with needles from which he hung heavy objects. There were also the Jewish tightrope walking sisters, (like his own Moishe) Pesa and Leah Rozentsvaug, the latter of whom married a Jewish circus clown, Itsik Gayler, and the former, the Jewish acrobat, Yankev Birnboym. Knowing all this provided some comfort to old Anshul, who hoped and prayed that his son would keep his balance while high up in the air without a safety net.

Moishe visited Patchentuch whenever he could, and Anshul remained patient and hopeful. Yes, Moishe was happy, he was earning a living and he had a family. Nonetheless, his father prayed that one day, God willing, his son would tire of the wire, and come down to return to the religious world of his fathers and forefathers, but only time would tell.

Efsha Retires

For several years Efsha Rabinovitz had been the leader and manager of the singing group, The Lucky Seven. Their performances on Sundays in the park were always well attended, and had quickly become a Patchentuch tradition. When the men had originally formed the group they were already old and, for the most part, retired, but their sudden fame kept them young at heart. Efsha was the oldest, however, and like Mayor Moishe Kapoyer, he had seriously begun to entertain thoughts of retiring as leader of the group.

"Oy, Efsha, you can't leave us," implored the men. "We need you. You are our leader," and so Efsha remained, for the time being. Privately, however, he had been talking to his cousin Henya Perelmuth, asking her to speak to her husband Louis, about taking over for him. Louis had music in his background, as did Efsha, and he was also retired, but considerably younger than Efsha.

After some coaxing and cajoling Louis agreed to give it a try. He was introduced to "The Lucky Seven", and he attended some rehearsals. Efsha explained to his group that Louis, who could sing, and who loved music, might be willing to assume the role of director and manager. None of the others, all of whom were older than Louis, was willing to assume the responsibility of leadership, and so they gratefully accepted Louis as their director. Efsha would continue to sing with the Lucky Seven, but he would no longer be required to shoulder the burden of being their leader.

As it turned out, Louis was a most effective manager, and often times, he brought along his son, Yehoshua Pinkhas Perelmutter, to join them, or to take the place of someone who was missing for one reason or another. Young Yehoshua had a beautiful voice, and in later years, when the family emigrated to America, young Yehoshua Pinkhus Perelmutter became the celebrated Jan Peerce of the Metropolitan Opera in New York, reflecting glory not just on himself, but on his origins as a performer in the Lucky Seven of Patchentuch.

Hennoch And Hodel's Pride

Hennoch and Hodel Pulches were proud of their only child, Chatchkel. He was a happy young boy but he was a bit ungainly, and a little slow: nevertheless his parents took pride in their son, certain that one day he would do wonderful things. As a young man Chatchkel went to work for his uncle, Yasher Koach, brother to his mother Hodel, in the business of barrel making. He proved to be a hard worker, and if one of Yasher's barrel molds failed, Chatchkel generously volunteered his hefty body as a mold around which the barrels could be formed until a replacement form could be made.

When Chatchel grew older he married Dvorah Shmookler, who was a good cook, and that made Chatchel a happily married man. He was a hard worker, and one of his duties around the workshop was sweeping up the floors after a long day of making barrels. In so doing, Chatchkel always found the remains of barrel making such as broken nails and assorted wires, cracked and discarded wooden staves and hoops for barrels, odd pieces of leather as well as other waste from the production process. He collected the bits and pieces that he found, and in the evenings, after eating the dinner that Dvorah had lovingly prepared, he tinkered with the castoff pieces to see what he could make of them. He created small trinkets from the detritus, and from the twisted nails he made bracelets and pins, from broken pieces of wood and other scraps he could make small toys, puppets, and small wooden figurines. He painted some of his trinkets in different colors, eventually accumulating a collection of small wonders, prompting Dvorah to make a suggestion.

"Chatchkel," she told her husband one night after dinner, what do you plan to do with all of these wonderful objects you have made?"

"I never really thought about it," he told her. "I just do it for the enjoyment of making something from nothing."

"But, my dear Chatchkel," she told him. "You can do better."

"How so?" he asked.

"I have an idea," she replied, and after a minute or so, she shared her thought with him.

"We have heard of "a barrel of fun", "a barrel of laughs" and "a barrel of monkeys," she told him.

"Yes we have all heard of those," Chatchkel laughed.

"How about "A Barrel of Chatchkel's Chatchkes?" Dvorah exclaimed.

Chatchkel was silent until his wife explained further.

"Perhaps on the first night of Chanukah just before candle lighting, the children of the town will gather with their parents in the town square, where you will be standing in the middle of the square with a large barrel filled with the chatchkes you have made, the bracelets, the toys, the puppets and the pins, and all the other wonderful and colorful trinkets. Every child will select one gift from the barrel, which will be named in honor and celebration of your work, "A Barrel of Chatchkel's Chatchkes." Chatchkel thought it was a wonderful idea, and so that is what they did. It soon became a yearly Chanukah tradition, which was, especially for the younger children, an occasion to happily celebrate the first night of the Festival of Lights in the little shtetl of Patchentuch. Years later when Chatchkel's puppets, called The Pulkes Puppets became famous throughout the region, Hennoch and Hodel, who always knew that their Chatchkel would accomplish great things, were happier and more proud of their son than they had ever imagined.

A Puppeteer In Patchentuch

Chatchkel Pulkes greatly enjoyed his hobby of creating things from the scraps he collected at the end of each day at the cooperage of his uncle Yasher Koach. Now, his pleasure had doubled, because each year at Chanukah he brought his barrel of the collectibles he had made to the market square, where the children of Patchentuch each received a small gift from the barrel. Chatchkel's joy at seeing their happy faces was perhaps even greater, if possible, than the joy of his little beneficiaries.

The item he most enjoyed making was not just a toy; it was a work of art, and like art of any kind, it brought pleasure to people. What could it be, this work of art? It was the puppet, or marionette, and over time, Chatchkel had become skilled as a wood carver. With a sharp knife to fashion recognizable forms from simple pieces of wood, he began carving faces, and then arms, legs and torsos that he connected together with strings so that his little people could move. By connecting these figures with more string to a handle of sorts, he was able to make them move. Dvorah, his wife, sewed little outfits for Chatchkel's wooden people, and it was at their kitchen table that the idea for "Pulkes Puppets" had been conceived.

Chatchkel and Dvorah decided to give their puppets names, as well as stories to go with those names. Together they created situations and fictional families that resided in Patchentuch, and with the strings, Chatchkel and Dvorah moved their little people accordingly. As they worked on their special project, they smiled and laughed, and Chatchkel found that he had never been happier.

During the days when he worked for his uncle, Chatchkel dreamed up scenarios for his people, all dressed up in Dvorah's clothes, and one day they decided to put on a performance for the children of the town. Everyone, and not just the children, but the adults, as well, loved the puppet shows. Patchentuch was now able to boast a puppet theatre of its own, an achievement, by the way, that the neighboring town of Schmertzburg could never duplicate.

Gimpel

Gimpel was an orphan child, who many years ago was taken in by Rose Kvetchernick, who had no husband or children, and Gimpel, now a young man, was in love. It was love at first sight when he first saw Bluma selling flowers in the market. From that moment she became the girl of his dreams. Simply put, Gimpel was smitten.

After spending many long hours at work, Gimpel's mind drifted off to thoughts of Bluma, and at night when he was in his bed, he thought of her. He seemed to slip out of his body, and fly out the window, and once free of restraint he soared over the village of Patchentuch. He flew over ramshackle rooftops and fields, climbing and diving in the air. He flew over the market, turning somersaults through low lying clouds. He soared over chicken coops and tree tops, drawing fresh air into his young lungs. He spread out his arms and rose higher in the sky as he pushed against the wind and did loop de loops. Gimpel's body had grown and his muscles had developed proportionately, so that flying had become easy. As he passed over Patchentuch he hoped Bluma might witness his fearless flight through the heavens. She would think him brave and wonderful and would love him as he loved her.

One clear night during the Hebrew month of Sivan when Gimpel was doing aerial acrobatics over Patchentuch, a sudden current of air jolted him from his reverie. Efforts to steady his body proved futile against the powerful winds and he struggled to keep control of his flight. To no avail, Gimpel fought the defiant gusts which wrapped around him, blowing him hither and yon against his will. With force and energy they pulled him farther and farther from Patchentuch.

It was not as if Gimpel had ever really spoken to Bluma. They had actually never had a real conversation, but for him she was a goddess. Her cheeks were rosy and smooth, and when she smiled, her dark eyes sparkled. Shiny brown curls framed her beautiful face, and when he passed by her he turned bright red around the neck and ears. Bluma had bewitched him, and his wish was that she could know it was he turning somersaults in the air. Now she would never know because he was being blown away. Rose Kvetchernick would surely worry when he did not return, and he hoped that Bluma would as well.

Farther and farther from Patchentuch Gimpel tumbled. Battered by gusts and currents he was tossed like a rag doll, until at last he lost consciousness. When he finally awoke he found himself lying on the shore of an ocean in a strange place he did not recognize. His head was spinning like a top, and his mind was a melange of confused images. His thoughts were of Rose, and of his home with her, but the image that mostly occupied his mind was that of Bluma, the love of his life.

Gimpel's first instinct was to lift himself up off the ground and fly back home to Patchentuch. Weak and confused he rose up from the rocky shore, but did not know where he was or in which direction home lay. Groggy and disoriented, and having staggered from the shore, Gimpel realized that he was hungry. He made his way into a nearby town of this nameless place, only to discover that he had been blown across the sea to America. As he wound his way through the street crowds, he was jostled and knocked to the ground. While on his hands and knees, he found a few random coins which he stuffed into his pocket, thinking that he might now be able to buy some bread and something to drink.

By day's end Gimpel had eaten some food, and despite his ragged clothes and disheveled appearance, he was able to persuade the owner of a small grocery store to give him a job and a place to sleep. Moishe Cohen spoke the Yiddish that Gimpel understood, and in return for room and board he offered the young man from Patchentuch a job in the store, as well as the added task of tutoring his son in Hebrew. Moishe instantly recognized that character and education lay beneath the bedraggled veneer of the young stranger, and that is how Gimpel came to dwell in the West End of Boston.

Gimpel worked hard, and he had recovered his bearings. He wanted to fly back home to Patchentuch, but when he puffed up his lungs to leap into the air and take flight, he discovered he had lost the gift. No matter how hard he tried, his body would not leave the ground. Without Bluma to inspire him, he could no longer fly. Without her he could no longer soar high above the earth and do somersaults in the air.

For two long years Gimpel worked in Moishe Cohen's store.
"Tea, coffee, cocoa, beans," was his daily mantra as the neighborhood wives and mothers asked the handsome young man from Patchentuch about the specials of the day.
"So what have you got for us today, Gimpel?"
"Tea, coffee, cocoa, beans," he told them as they laughed and pinched his cheeks. He had grown older, however, and no longer liked having his cheeks pinched. After store hours he continued to tutor Moishe Cohen's son, and under his tutelage the young boy learned his lessons well. All the while Gimpel longed for home, and the time when he would have saved enough money for passage.

At last that day did arrive, and as Gimpel boarded his ship, parting tears were shed by all. He had grow fond of the Cohens, and they of him. They had been good to him, treating him like family, and Gimpel would never forget their kindness.

For weeks that seemed like years Gimpel felt seasick. His stomach heaved and churned in counterpoint to the crashing waves that lashed at the ship. He wanted to die, and it was only thoughts of Patchentuch that sustained him. As the sea tossed the ship like a cork, Gimpel closed his eyes, and for brief moments was flying over the beautiful hills of home. Down he swooped and around he looped. He would find Bluma, and they would be together. He would teach her to lift herself off the ground and fly with him. Together they would expand the limits of what was possible and push beyond the ordinary. With her at his side he would become more. As he made his way across the ocean Gimpel never lost hope. To help pay for his passage he had signed on for the job of cleaning decks, which he did in all kinds of weather. Slowly he became acclimated to the rolling rhythm of the vessel, and the swells that had once made him ill now bothered him less. He had even learned to keep down his food. As the weeks passed he adjusted to life on board, occupying himself with thoughts of home and Rose Kvetchernick, but mostly about Bluma.

One day, as he scrubbed the decks, a sudden chill interrupted Gimpel's thoughts over life and his future. He looked up to see a darkening sky on the horizon toward which they sailed. As the seas grew rougher the ship began to dip and rise. The sky, now black, erupted into wild torrents of rain. Gimpel could see nothing except for brief, frightening flashes of lightning that illuminated the deck, sailors scrambling to hold on to anything that would keep them from being swept overboard. As the ship rolled, Gimpel was hurled toward the side of the deck, where he struck a railing and grabbed hold until the railing broke from the force of his body. He held on until he and the stout railing were no longer attached to the ship, and he found himself being tossed about in the angry ocean. A flash of lightning revealed his ship, some distance away now, floundering and not likely to survive.

Gimpel thought he would have preferred to go down in the company of his shipmates, condemned as they were, rather than drown alone in this savage storm. He realized he was still holding tightly to the fragment of wooden railing that he'd held onto when he was thrown from the ship. He had never experienced such a sensation, not even when flying. One moment he was in a deep trough, and the next he was involuntarily hurled to the crest of a wave at least fifty feet in height. He held on for what seemed like an eternity, but was actually only a few hours. Soon, he sensed that the distances between peak and trough had begun to lessen and the seas were less angry. The grey green waves had become smaller and the distance between them increased. He also noticed that the sky had begun to lighten and a hint of sunlight was visible through the clouds.

Hope swelled within his heart. Might he actually survive this turbulent storm that had surely taken his ship and its crew? Then, like the rise and fall of the ocean waves, his heart sank. He was in the middle of a great sea, alive only because of the fragment of railing he had grasped. Who could save him from this vast expanse of rolling water?

Some time later, Gimpel opened his eyes only to discover that he was becalmed. Had he slept, still hanging on to the railing? Night had come and gone, and it was now bright daylight. The sun beat down on him, but he felt no better because he was keenly aware of his predicament. He was again lost, but this time would probably be his last.

It turned out that this was not the last time that Gimpel was lost. The Lord had not intended for him to die quite yet because a passing ship spotted him clinging to the floating piece of railing and rescued him. For days he suffered from delirium, and weeks later when the ship docked at Southampton, the crew left him off at the dock. Still weak, but recovering, Gimpel signed on to another ship bound for France. He worked as a deck hand on this vessel which took him through the Strait of Gibralter, past Spain and Portugal to Marseilles. He then boarded a freighter which carried him past Sardinia and Corsica, eventually bringing him to Messina, Sicily.

As Gimpel sailed from port to port the years passed. He traveled to Crete in the Aegean Sea, and into Istanbul, through the

Dardanelles, and eventually to the Black Sea and Odessa. He was twenty four years old when he boarded a river boat up the Dniester River to Kishinev. He felt like flotsam in the world, a man without a compass. The sound of ocean had been his constant companion, its rush filling his ears and soothing his lonely spirit. He had often wandered the shores of distant ports in which he found himself climbing over jagged rocks and casting his eye out over the horizon. Each destination had brought him closer, yet still he was so far. Rock cliffs stood like sentinels on foreign shores, and for Gimpel each port was another mountain climbed. No matter how far he traveled, however, the place he sought seemed just beyond. Sunsets came and went, and their passing had made home seem even more inaccessible. The homesickness was a pain in his heart, reminding him of how far he still was from home and from those he loved.

Finally he had reached the Dniester, and his goal was in sight. It was spring, and hope was in the air. He had reached his destination, he thought, as he made his way toward Patchentuch, to Rose Kvetchernick and to Bluma. Suddenly a gust of wind from the sea blew in, and Gimpel surrendered to the force which filled his coat like a sail, lifting him up off the ground and into the sky. God was surely the source of this wind, he thought, and would keep him safe, and so he surrendered to the pull and he soared with its currents. He rose and dove with the breeze as he spread out his arms and did loop de loops. Back toward Patchentuch he flew, filling his lungs with fresh air and rising to the heights that would lead him to his salvation.

Through God's grace Gimpel arrived home, was reunited with Rose Kvetchernick, and when he fully recovered from his long ordeal, he set out to find Bluma.....and when he awoke in the morning from this wonderful, yet terrible dream, that had seemed so real, he really did seek out Bluma, and he introduced himself in person.

Printed in the United States
by Baker & Taylor Publisher Services